# Finding True Friends

WRITTEN AND ILLUSTRATED BY
PILAR MARIE

ISBN: 978-0-578-82702-5

# DEDICATION

This book is dedicated to children everywhere. Believe in yourself, and remember that you are loved.

With two kicks, a hop, and a skip,
Rocky the donkey set off on a trip.

Out of his stall and across the barn,
through the doors and out on the farm.

He passed two tractors and a plow,
when out jumped Beth, a small brown cow.

This scared the poor little donkey,
who tripped and yelled out "Haw Hee!"

Beth the cow looked at Rocky.
"Don't you mean Hee Haw, not Haw Hee, donkey?"

"No," he replied, "it's what I say.
I wouldn't be me if I talked another way!"

Beth looked sad: "I'm different, too.
I say Oooom instead of Moo."

"The others all make fun of me,
but with kind friends, I would be happy!"

"Oh," said Rocky, "that's happened to me, too. I will never laugh at you."

"Come with me, and don't be sad.
You're one of a kind, which should make you glad!"

The two new friends went on their way,
past the fields with bales of hay.

When out from a bush Bob the rooster flew,
in a blur of green and red and blue.

This scared both the rooster and the other two:

Doodle Cocka Doo!

The rooster looked at the cow and the donkey.
"Don't you mean Moo and Hee Haw,
not Haw Hee?"

"No," Beth replied, "it's what we say.
We wouldn't be us if we talked another way!"

Bob looked sad: "I'm different, too.
I say Doodle Cocka Doo, not Cocka Doodle Doo!"

"The others all make fun of me,
but with kind friends, I would be happy!"

"Oh," said Beth, "that's happened to us, too.
We will never laugh at you!"

"Come with us, and don't be sad.
You're one of a kind, which should make you glad!"

The three new friends continued on,
past a house and across a lawn.

When Bill the cat fell from a tree,
scaring both Bill and the other three.

OW
ME!

The cat looked at the cow, the rooster, and the donkey.
"Don't you mean Moo, Cocka Doodle Doo, and Hee Haw, not Haw Hee?"

"No," Bob replied, "it's what we say.
We wouldn't be us if we talked another way!"

Bill looked sad: "I'm different, too.
I say Ow Me, not Meow or Mew!"

"The others all make fun of me,
but with kind friends, I would be happy!"

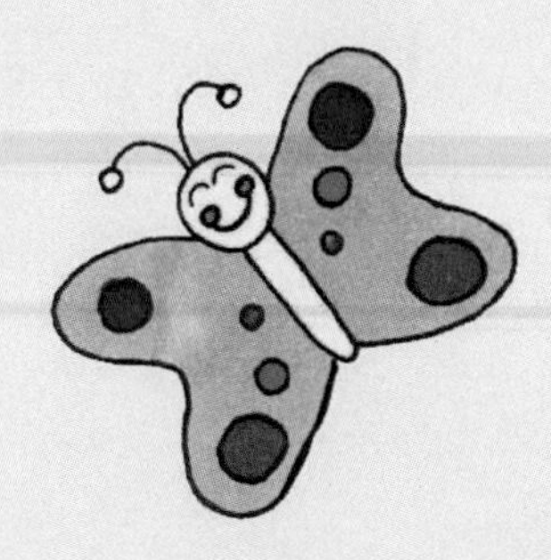

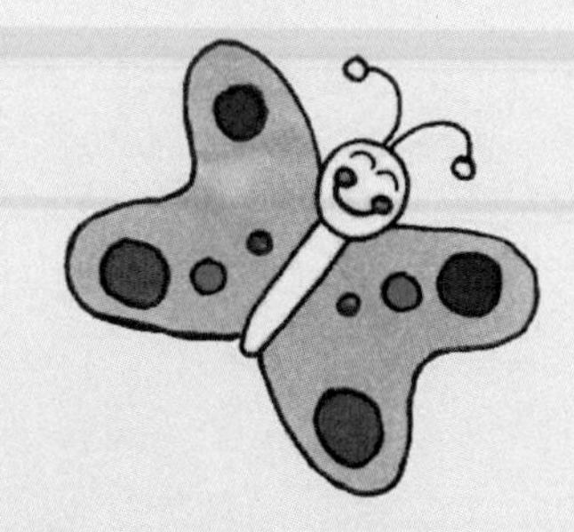

"Oh," said Bob, "that's happened to us, too. We will never laugh at you!"

"Come with us, and don't be sad.
You're one of a kind, which should make you glad!"

The four new friends walked side by side,
no longer sad, with heads held high.

Singing proudly as they went,
smiling wide, feeling content.

When they ran straight into Sour Sully,
a plump spotted pig and a bit of a bully.

She snarled, "Look at you backwards four,
making all our eardrums sore."

"Can't you talk the way you should?
The rest of us sure wish you would!"

Beth, Bob, and Bill all cried,
as they stopped where they stood,
side by side.

But Rocky went up to his friends,
wiped their tears, and smiled as he said:

"Mean words hurt. That is true.
But, friends, I like you just for you."

"It doesn't matter how you look,
or matter how you talk,
or matter how you sound as we sing on a walk."

What matters is something we've all got...
LOVE for one another,
and my friends, that's a lot!"

And suddenly all of the animals knew
just who they should be listening to.

And, so, they each sang out once more,
far louder than they had before!

For now they could clearly see
that they had kind friends and were very happy.

THE END

# THANK YOU FOR YOUR SUPPORT

Thank you for reading Finding True Friends. If you enjoyed it, please consider leaving a review. I appreciate each and every comment.

# ABOUT THE AUTHOR

Pilar Marie is an army wife and a mother to four young children. She has bachelor's degrees in English and science and a master's in elementary education.

She can be reached at pilarmariebooks@gmail.com with any questions or special requests.

Made in the USA
Monee, IL
04 January 2021

56524038R00021